Please renew or return items by the date shown on your receipt

www.hertsdirect.org/libraries

Renewals and enquiries:	0300 123 4049
Textphone for hearing or speech impaired	0300 123 4041

Hertfordshire

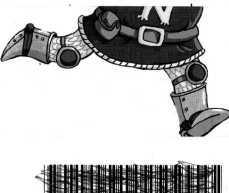

For Sir Gabriel the Great, storyteller extraordinaire

S. P-H.

For my wonderful wife Francesca

I. S.

EGMONT
We bring stories to life

Book Band: Turquoise

First published in Great Britain 2014
by Egmont UK Ltd
The Yellow Building, 1 Nicholas Road, London W11 4AN
Text copyright © Smriti Prasadam-Halls 2014
Illustrations copyright © Ian Smith 2014
The author and illustrator have asserted their moral rights.
ISBN 978 1 4052 6211 8
www.egmont.co.uk
A CIP catalogue record for this title is available from the British Library.
Printed in Singapore.
51392/1

EGMONT LUCKY COIN

Our story began over a century ago, when seventeen-year-old
Egmont Harald Petersen found a coin in the street.

He was on his way to buy a flyswatter, a small hand-operated
printing machine that he then set up in his tiny apartment.

The coin brought him such good luck that today Egmont has
offices in over 30 countries around the world. And that lucky
coin is still kept at the company's head offices in Denmark.

Norman the Naughty Knight

Smriti Prasadam-Halls

Illustrated by Ian Smith

Blue Bananas

Norman Knight loved stories. Long ones, short ones, horrid ones, hairy ones, he loved them all.

And more than reading them, he loved TELLING them.

On Monday, Norman told the queen
a story.

'Mum! Look! A blackbird is
flying away with Cook's nose!' he said.
'Heavens!' cried the queen, and she
raced down to the kitchen.

But when the queen got there, she found Cook cheerfully feeding cake crumbs to the birds, while her plump little nose sat safely in the middle of her face.

'That was naughty, Norman!' panted the queen crossly.

'Sorry, Mum!' giggled Norman.

On Tuesday, Norman woke the king up with a story.

'Dad! Wake up! We're being attacked!'

'War!' cried the king, flinging on bits of armour as he flew out of his bedchamber.

Let me at 'em!

At the bottom of the stairs he saw a line of tiny toy soldiers.

'Norman!' shouted the king.

'Sorry, Dad!' chuckled Norman.

And on Wednesday, Norman told his brother a story.

'Henry! Come quick! There's a shark in the moat!'

'Yikes!' cried Prince Henry, racing out with all his weapons ready.

Sh-sh-shark?

But it was only a big fish with a pointy fin.

'Norman!' fumed Henry.

'Sorry, Henry!' snorted Norman.

And so the days went on.

Thursday . . .

Friday . . .

Saturday . . .

Sunday . . .

And by Dragon Day,
everyone in the castle was
completely fed up with
Norman and his stories.

'Well, Norman!' said the king. 'I'm afraid you must stay at home today. You've been too naughty to come dragoning with us!'

'But Dad!' begged Norman. 'Dragon Day is the best. I'll be really good. I PROMISE!'

'Guarding the castle is an important job for any young knight,' said the king. 'Do it well and maybe you can come next time!'

'And,' added the queen sternly, 'DON'T BE NAUGHTY, Norman!'

Then away they galloped, leaving
poor Norman feeling very glum and
gloomy.

It's dragoning
time!

'It isn't fair!' said Norman miserably.
'Nothing exciting will happen at
boring old home!'

Just then, there was a loud rat-a-tat-tat at the door of Creaky Castle.

Norman eagerly ran to open it.

'Friend or foe?' he called out in his bravest voice.

'Friend!' It was Henry. He'd forgotten to go to the loo.

'Enter!' sighed Norman crossly, sliding open the heavy oak door.

Then he cried, 'Look out, Henry ... there's a massive, scary dragon behind you!'

'Where?' cried Henry, instantly drawing his sword. 'Stand back, Norman!'

Oh, Norman!

'Whoops, not really,' chuckled Norman. 'Tee hee ... But I like your moves!'

Quite soon there was another rat-a-tat-tat at the door of Creaky Castle.

'Friend or foe?' yelled Norman.

'Friend!' called back a familiar voice.

'Enter!' said Norman again, opening the door.

'Whoops, just left my sword in the loo!' It was Henry again.

'Watch out! Dragon!' yelled Norman.

'It's about to pounce on you!'

'Where?' cried Henry, raising his shield to defend himself.

'Oh dear, 'fraid it must have gone,' chuckled Norman naughtily. 'But good defence action, Henry!'

Soon there was yet another rat-a-tat-tat at the door of Creaky Castle. 'This is getting SILLY, Henry,' shouted Norman, flinging the castle door wide open. 'ENTER!' he yelled. But it wasn't Henry.

There on the doorstep stood a real,

scaly,
smoky,
fire-breathing
dragon!

Don't mind if I do,' said the dragon. 'But, by the way, my name's not Henry.'

Yikes!

'ARGH! Help!' yelled Norman, looking round desperately for anything that could save him. 'Henry! Come back! Come BACK!'

'Shhhhhh' whispered the dragon
loudly, putting its finger to its lip and
accidentally breathing a bit of fire
on it. 'Ouch!'

Norman was terrified. There was only
one thing that a brave knight could
possibly do . . .

He climbed on top of the chandelier and
closed his eyes as tightly as he could.

Maybe the horrible dragon won't see me up here! he thought.

Turn around!

At that moment, Henry appeared in the doorway of Creaky Castle.

'Norman! Where are you? I thought I heard the sound of yelling,' he called. 'Oh for goodness' sake, what are you doing up there?'

'Henry! Henry! Quick! Come and rescue me . . . there's a DRAGON!' screamed Norman.

'Get down and stop being ridiculous,' said Henry huffily. 'I thought you really needed something, but it's just that silly old story, AGAIN!'

'But Henry! Look! The dragon's right there, behind you!'

'Not falling for that one again!' laughed Henry, shaking his head. 'See you later!' And he cheerfully slammed the door behind him.

All was quiet in Creaky Castle. Norman gingerly opened one eye and looked around. He couldn't see the dragon anywhere. Hurrah! The dragon was gone!

'Hello!' boomed a voice behind Norman's head.

'Argh!' screeched Norman, almost falling off the chandelier.

The dragon had flown up behind him and was flapping its enormous wings. 'Would you like some company? I'm actually quite nice, you know.'

Norman peered at the dragon and the dragon peered back. The dragon didn't try to set fire to Norman, or fight him, or bite him.

Norman decided it was time to get over the shock of having a dragon in the castle. So, at last, he climbed down from on top of the chandelier.

The dragon plopped down beside him.

Hmmm, thought Norman. He'd noticed that the dragon really DID seem quite friendly. 'You don't look much like a scary dragon,' he said.

'And you don't look much like a scary knight,' said the dragon.

'Good point,' said Norman. 'But you should be out fighting knights. It's Dragon Day!'

'Well, a very fierce family started chasing me, so I thought I'd come and hide in here. I'm not very good at being a dragon, you see,' the dragon sighed.

'I'm too small to be scary, my roar isn't loud enough and I don't really want to fight knights. I'd much rather play with them.'

'Well, if you're absolutely sure you aren't going to swallow me up, then, if you like . . . you can play with me!' said Norman happily.

'Delightful!' said the dragon. 'But first, do you mind if I light a fire? It's freezing in here!'

'Creaky Castle is always cold,' said Norman. 'Cook hates making the fires because they just go out again, so we all wear an extra jumper instead.'

'We'll soon fix that. Climb aboard!' said the dragon, and they zoomed around the castle, lighting fires in every room.

Next the dragon, whose name was
Doris, told Norman she was hungry.
'Let's see what's cooking, shall we?' she
said, and they sailed down to the kitchen.

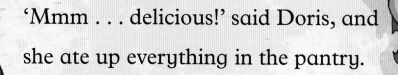

'Mmm . . . delicious!' said Doris, and she ate up everything in the pantry.

Next they went into the queen's dressing room.

'What fun!' exclaimed Doris, draping herself from head to toe in twinkling tiaras and ruby rings.

Then they played in Henry's room.
'I've always wanted to have a proper
look around a castle. You don't get
much time when you're capturing
princesses!' Doris said, rifling through
swords and shields and helmets.

So pointy!

Finally, they had a little sit down on
the royal thrones in the great hall.

'This is the best day I've ever had,' sighed Doris. 'I wish I lived in a real castle, like you.'

At that moment they heard footsteps. Norman's family were back.

'Doris! Come and meet my . . .' said Norman, but Doris had disappeared.

'Hello, Norman! I hope you've been good. Did you guard the castle well and keep dangerous intruders out?' asked the king.

'Erm . . . yes, Dad, sort of!' said Norman.

'Excellent!' said the king.

'Did you fight any dragons?' asked Norman.

'No, not much luck there,' said the king grumpily. 'We did spot a small one but it flew away when it saw us! Very strange!'

All was quiet for about a minute. Then things became very, very noisy.

'Where's all the food?'

yelled Cook.

'Where's my jewellery?'

yelled the queen.

'Where's my bow and arrows?'

yelled Henry.

'Where's my crown?'

yelled the king.

'NORMAN?!' they all yelled together.

'It wasn't me!' cried Norman. 'But I can explain. You see, while you were out I had tea with a dragon. She's brilliant and her name is Doris.'

'Impossible!' said the queen crossly.

'Ridiculous!' said Henry.

'Not ANOTHER story, Norman!' moaned the king, rolling his eyes.

'Oh dear, Norman,' said Doris.

Everyone looked round.

'ARGH! A dragon!' they all shrieked,
jumping out of their skins as they
saw Doris.

'ARGH!' shrieked Doris, jumping
out of her skin because everyone was
looking at her.

'YOU SEE! I told you so,' said Norman happily. 'This is Doris. Please can we keep her?' he asked, when everyone had got over the shock and climbed down from on top of the chandelier.

'She *has* been a bit naughty, but she's also been good. Look, she's lit all the fires AND she's kept me out of trouble all day!'

'Well, it would be nice not
to make the fires any more!'
said Cook.

'It would be nice to
be warm again,'
said the king.

'It would be nice to
have another girl in
the house,' said the queen.

'And she *is* rather
pretty,' said Henry.

'Best of all,' chuckled the king, 'she's naughtier than you, Norman, so at least we won't have to worry about you and your stories any more. You'll be too busy keeping an eye on Doris!'

'Hooray!' cheered the rest of the family.

'Hooray!' cheered Norman and Doris.

And everyone laughed.

Creaky Castle has got a new name.
It's called Cosy Castle now. If you visit,
you'll be sure to get a warm welcome
and lots of lovely food.

The castle speciality is Dragon-Fired Doughnuts, baked by Doris, the friendly pet dragon.

And if you want to hear how it all happened, just ask Norman . . . He'll tell you the whole story!